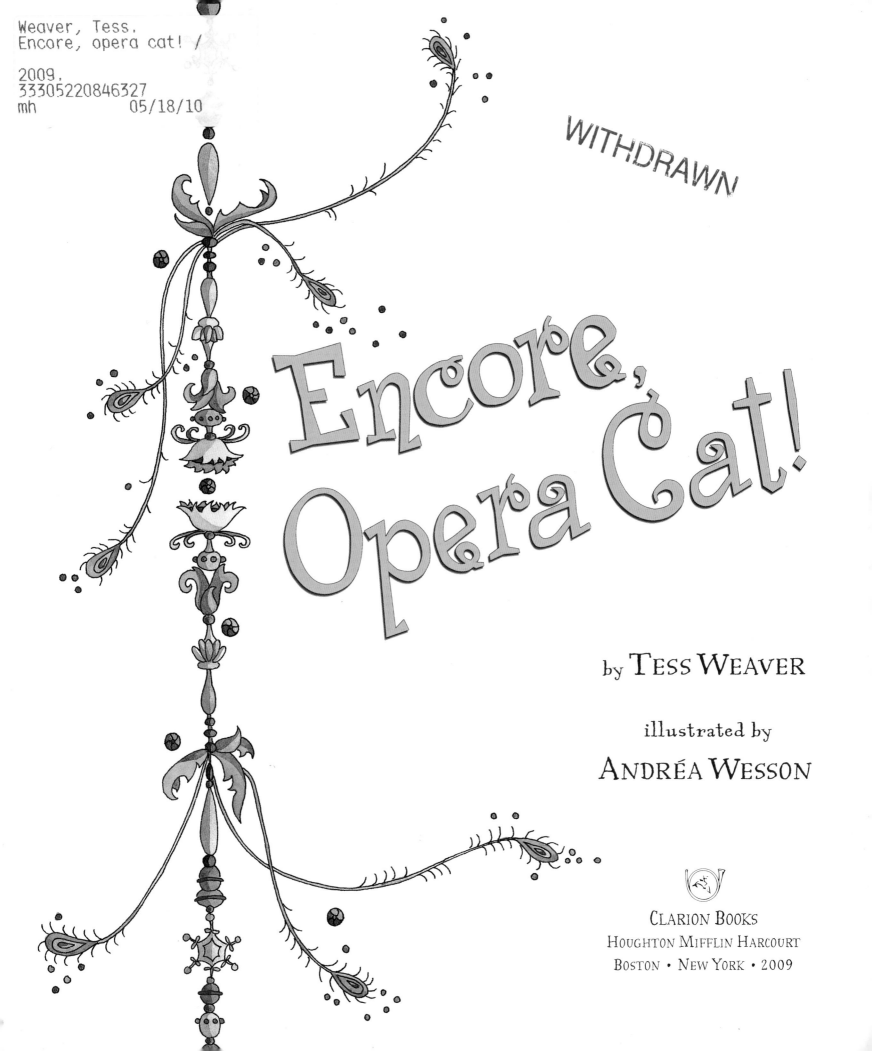

Encore, Opera Cat!

by TESS WEAVER

illustrated by

ANDRÉA WESSON

CLARION BOOKS
HOUGHTON MIFFLIN HARCOURT
BOSTON • NEW YORK • 2009

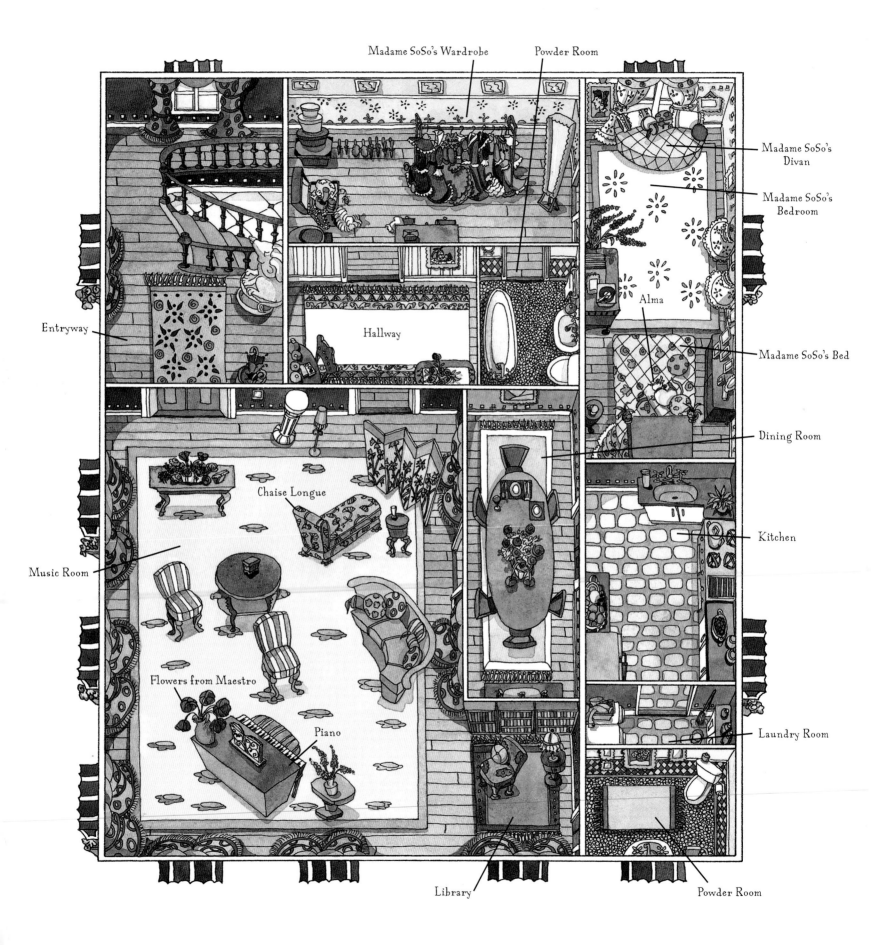

Madame SoSo's Wardrobe

Powder Room

Madame SoSo's Divan

Madame SoSo's Bedroom

Alma

Madame SoSo's Bed

Entryway

Hallway

Dining Room

Kitchen

Music Room

Chaise Longue

Laundry Room

Flowers from Maestro

Piano

Library

Powder Room

For Mary Jo, Kathy, Janie, Bob, and L.G.;
and for Holly, without whom . . .
–T.W.

For John, Ben, and Gillian
–A.W.

Clarion Books
215 Park Avenue South, New York, NY 10003
Text copyright © 2009 by Thérèse Gullickson
Illustrations copyright © 2009 by Andréa Wesson

The illustrations were executed in watercolor.
The text was set in 22-point Aunt Mildred.

For information about permission to reproduce selections from
this book, write to Permissions, Houghton Mifflin Harcourt
Publishing Company, 215 Park Avenue South, New York, NY 10003.

Clarion Books is an imprint of Houghton Mifflin Harcourt Publishing Company.

www.clarionbooks.com

Manufactured in China

Library of Congress Catalog-in-Publication Data

Weaver, Tess
Encore, opera cat / by Tess Weaver; illustrated by Andréa Wesson.
p. cm.
Summary: Alma the cat loves to sing and dreams of one day singing on stage with
her mistress, Madame SoSo, an opera singer.
ISBN 978-0-547-14647-8
[1. Cats–Fiction. 2. Opera–Fiction. 3. Singers–Fiction. 4. Italy–Fiction.] I. Wesson, Andréa,
ill. II. Title.

PZ7.W3655En 2009
[E]–dc22

2008040811

LEO 10 9 8 7 6 5 4 3 2 1

Alma and Madame SoSo lived in Italy, where each of them sang opera. Madame SoSo sang in front of large audiences. Alma sang in Madame SoSo's apartment. They were both happy with this arrangement.

Or so it seemed.

Secretly, Alma dreamed of singing onstage.
Every catnap, every summer slumber, every winter's
dream was always the same: Alma in the spotlight,
thrilling people with her voice.

But what would Maestro say if he knew her secret?
Would people laugh if she went onstage?
Could a small cat sing about love?

Each day Alma practiced, her voice grew stronger
and brighter. One morning, she sang a very high note.
"La-a-a-a-a!" Her voice filled the apartment with a
shimmering silver tone that shattered Madame
SoSo's water glass.

"Alma," said Madame SoSo. "Your voice is too big
for this tiny apartment. We can't hide your
talent any longer. Let's tell Maestro your secret."

Alma sighed so musically, it sounded
as if she was singing
"Yesssss!"

Later that day, Madame SoSo tried to tell Maestro the exciting news. "I've discovered a new singer," she announced.

"There's no time for talk," answered Maestro. "We've got a concert in Switzerland in one week."

"But—" began Madame SoSo.

"Later, cara!" said Maestro.

The next day, Madame SoSo tried again. Maestro was too busy to listen . . . and too distracted to pay attention.

The following day, Madame SoSo suggested a duet.

"Impossible!" Maestro answered. "You can't sing with someone else. Only *your* voice stirs my soul!"

"Maestro," pleaded Madame SoSo, "please listen to this singer."
She tried to coax Alma to the center of the room, but Alma knew
Maestro didn't want to hear her. She slipped behind the door.

Maestro shook his head. "Sometimes I worry about you, cara,"
he said, checking to see if she had a fever. "A little singing will
make you feel better, yes?"

11

That night, Alma and Madame SoSo hatched a plan to
surprise Maestro—and the whole world—with a duet at
the concert in Switzerland. Alma agreed only when
Madame SoSo let her choose a mask . . . a wig . . . and a costume.

Alma liked the idea of dressing up. No one would guess she
was a cat unless she took off her mask!

NO PETS ALLOWED!

Soon it was time to go to Switzerland
for the big performance. The day of the trip,
Alma and Madame SoSo arrived at the train
station with their luggage. When they tried
to board the train, the conductor pointed to a
sign that read: NO PETS ALLOWED!

13

Before Madame SoSo could hide her friend, Alma was pulled away.

"No!" shrieked Madame SoSo. "Alma is practically human."

"That's what they all say," answered the conductor.

"But," whimpered Madame SoSo. "She's special!"

"She can ride in back," said the conductor.

"Sing, Alma!" shouted Madame SoSo.

But it was too late; Alma was gone.

"Your little cat will be fine," said Maestro. "It's you I'm worried about."

As Maestro helped Madame SoSo onto the train, Alma settled onto a lumpy mailbag.

It was a long, cold ride.

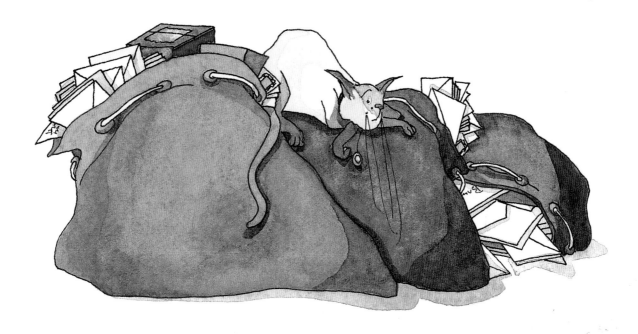

At the station,
Madame SoSo had to wait in
a long line to collect Alma.

When they finally arrived
at the opera house,
everyone was in an uproar.
"Where have you been?"
the director cried.
"Hurry!" said the
stage manager.

Madame SoSo rushed into her dressing room.
She began to warm up her voice, "La-la-la-LA-la-la-la."

As she applied her makeup, she saw that Alma was trembling.
"Don't be afraid," she whispered. "You'll be wonderful."
But Alma wasn't trembling in fear. She was shaking
with excitement.

Madame SoSo helped Alma into her gown and tucked
her pointed ears under her wig. Once Alma held the
mask over her face, she was ready.

A knock came at the door. "Two minutes!"
Madame SoSo glued on her eyelashes and headed
for the stage. Alma stepped into the shadows to listen
for her cue.

While she was waiting in the wings, she
heard a stage hand say, "Hey, who's that?"
Who? Alma looked around.
"Is that what I think it is?" asked another.
Alma looked up just as someone tried to grab her.

She dashed behind some heavy ropes and hid in a
small room. Her heart was racing. They knew
she was a cat! But how?

She looked at herself in a dusty mirror. Her
wig was on straight. Her gown was stunning.
But . . . she could see it now: her whiskers were
showing! Her paws didn't
look like hands. And her tail
was hard to hide.

Alma's disguise didn't work.

Madame SoSo's voice echoed through the concert hall, reminding Alma to come onstage. "*Alma, mia!*" she sang. Alma hesitated. Would anyone listen to a cat sing about love?

"*Alma, mia!*" sang Madame SoSo once again.

Sadly, Alma took off her mask. No matter what she wore, she'd always be a cat. She walked through the long, dark hallway and stepped . . .

. . . into the light.

If she wanted to be a singer, she couldn't hide
any longer. She looked at the astonished crowd,
took a deep breath, and bravely began to sing.
"Dolce ristoro!"

The musicians stopped with a loud drum beat. Alma kept singing.

People stood up . . . pointed . . . giggled. Alma kept singing.

Maestro's mouth popped open. He swayed forward . . . and backward. He dropped his baton!

Alma kept singing . . . beautifully.

24

Then Madame SoSo joined Alma's song.

"Io ti stringo in questo sen."

Soon their voices blended so sweetly, the heavenly tones soared through the opera house, making the audience gasp and the chandeliers ring.

"Ooooooooohhhh!" sighed the crowd.

"Aaaaaaaaaahhhhh!" they breathed.

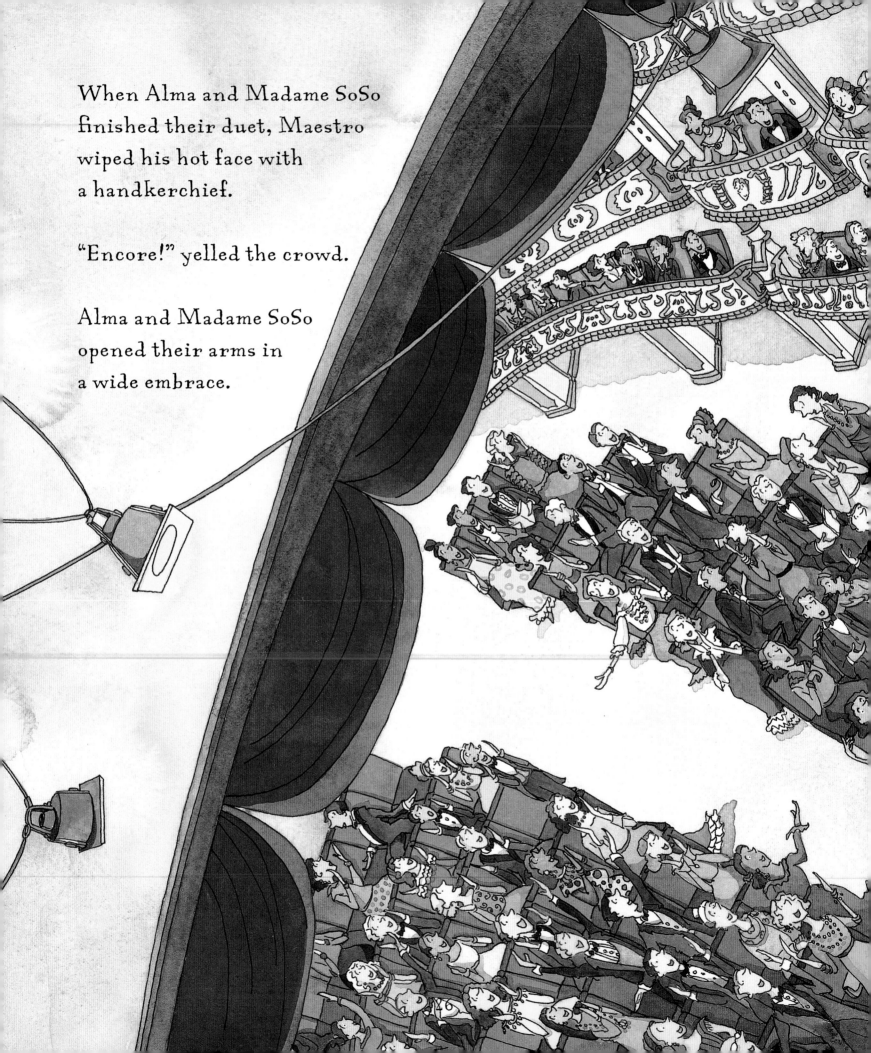

When Alma and Madame SoSo finished their duet, Maestro wiped his hot face with a handkerchief.

"Encore!" yelled the crowd.

Alma and Madame SoSo opened their arms in a wide embrace.

After the concert, Maestro appeared at Madame SoSo's
dressing room. "I—I—I—," he stammered. "She—she . . . you!"
He gazed deeply into Madame SoSo's eyes. "I've never heard
anyone sing about love with such passion. Why didn't you
tell me?" he asked.

"You wouldn't listen," Madame SoSo answered softly.
Maestro sighed and kissed Alma's paw.
Then he held Madame SoSo's hand.
"Cara," he said, "I'm listening now.
Tell me all about it."

So they told him . . . everything.

Maestro was so enchanted, he put their story to music. Opera has never been the same since!